GOING WILD

Amazing Animal Adventures

At the Poles

with Brian Keating

BRIAN KEATING'S AMAZING ANIMAL ADVENTURES

Getting to It All

Canaries of the Ocean

Muskox Island

Superbears of the North

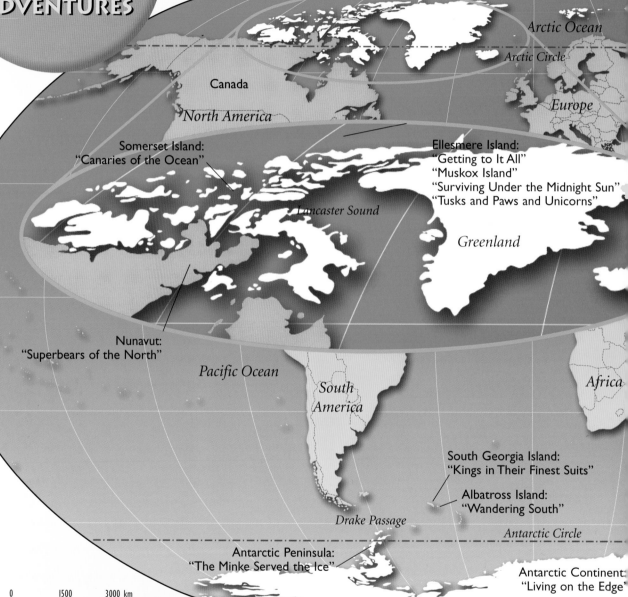

Arctic Ocean

Arctic Circle

Canada

North America

Europe

Somerset Island:
"Canaries of the Ocean"

Ellesmere Island:
"Getting to It All"
"Muskox Island"
"Surviving Under the Midnight Sun"
"Tusks and Paws and Unicorns"

Lancaster Sound

Greenland

Nunavut:
"Superbears of the North"

Pacific Ocean

South America

Africa

South Georgia Island:
"Kings in Their Finest Suits"

Albatross Island:
"Wandering South"

Drake Passage

Antarctic Circle

Antarctic Peninsula:
"The Minke Served the Ice"

Antarctic Continent:
"Living on the Edge"

N

0   1500   3000 km

Tusks and Paws and Unicorns

Living on the Edge

The Minke Served the Ice

Wandering Sout

Surviving Under
the Midnight Sun

Kings in Their
Finest Suits

TABLE OF CONTENTS

Asia

Indian Ocean

Pacific
Ocean

Southern Ocean

A NATURALIST IS BORN

I was born in Medicine Hat, Alberta, but lived there for only the first 6 years of my life. My sister was born deaf and my parents wanted her to learn how to speak, so we moved to New York. In those days, the Lexington School for the Deaf in New York City was the only place that taught deaf kids how to speak. So, in a 1957 Chevy and a homemade trailer that looked like a silver teardrop, my parents drove with four kids under the age of 8 to New York.

I developed my interest in birdwatching in New York, my home for 11 years. I'll never forget a day of discovery when I was 12 years old. I was walking in the rain on a trail in the woods. I was trying to stay dry under a garbage pail lid I had found, and suddenly a scarlet tanager landed on the tree in front of me. I remember gasping aloud at the sight and I was hooked. Birdwatching became a passion that later branched into all areas of natural history. My parents encouraged my interest in nature and sent me to summer school courses on marine biology, archaeology, and dinosaurs.

After our family moved back to Canada, I went to Lakeland College in Vermilion, Alberta, and later to Brandon University, in Manitoba, to study fish and wildlife. In my spare time I climbed mountains and went skiing, camping, and hiking. When I graduated, I got a job as a naturalist in southern British Columbia and couldn't believe my good fortune. Here I was being paid to learn more about nature!

I met Dee while we were both working with the Canadian Wildlife Service. We were new naturalists. Our working relationship slowly developed into a weekend hiking relationship, which eventually led to our marriage. We're still best friends to this day.

When Dee was accepted at the University of Calgary to study medicine, I became director of the Calgary Zoo's education department. I had that job for 15 years. I now direct the zoo's Conservation Outreach Program, which allows me to help conservation projects around the world. This kind of outreach is what I believe a zoo's primary mission should be. A good zoo does important conservation work and gets people interested in nature. Many of the world's biologists will tell you they had their first inspiration at a zoo.

Your Own Backyard Adventure
Build Your Own Plant Press

In "Surviving Under the Midnight Sun" I talk about how I built my own plant press so I could start identifying Arctic plants on Ellesmere Island. You can find out more about plants in your own backyard by using a plant identification book from your local library and building your own plant press, following the directions below. Keep in mind that each plant you choose to press is a life that deserves respect.

You will need:
- a large piece of cardboard
- four thick rubber bands
- sheets of old newspaper
- scissors
- flowers and leaves

How to make the press:
1. Cut the cardboard into four 10 cm x 10 cm (4 in. x 4 in.) squares.
2. Cut the newspaper into twelve 10 cm x 10 cm (4 in. x 4 in.) squares.
3. Place four sheets of newspaper in between each cardboard piece.
4. Place the four rubber bands around the outside of the cardboard, so that the contents are secure and tight.

Pressing plants:
1. Gather the flowers and leaves that you would like to identify.
2. Cut the plants so that they are no bigger than the press itself.
3. Separate the sheets of newspaper and neatly place the plant in between four sheets of paper (two sheets on top, two on the bottom). Spread out the flower petals and leaves.
4. Place the newspaper between two pieces of cardboard.
5. Repeat this process until the plant press is full.
6. Secure the press with rubber bands—the tighter, the better.
7. Place the press in a dry place and do not open for at least 48 hours. (More time would be better.)
8. After 48 hours, you may remove the plants and mount them on paper.

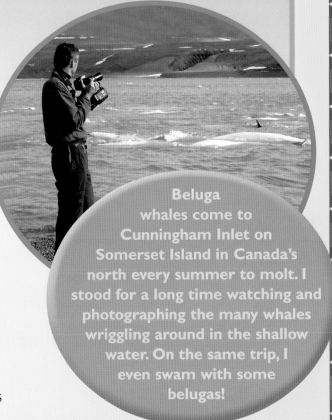

Beluga whales come to Cunningham Inlet on Somerset Island in Canada's north every summer to molt. I stood for a long time watching and photographing the many whales wriggling around in the shallow water. On the same trip, I even swam with some belugas!

Last year the Calgary Zoo supported a dozen conservation projects around the world, including a fund to save the albatross from extinction. You will read more about these amazing birds later in this book. I hope you will see in these stories some of the amazing people, places, plants, and animals that have inspired me to learn more about nature and to seek the world's wild spaces. Maybe something in these stories will inspire you, too.

GETTING
to IT ALL

When I was 21, I landed a job at a weather station called Eureka on the Fosheim Peninsula of Ellesmere Island. It was a summer handyman job, which meant I was the guy who swept up after everybody and did the dishes and odd jobs. I was excited, not because of the job but because of where the job was. Ellesmere Island is in Canada's High Arctic, on the top of the world. I had started backpacking a number of years before that and I'd been birdwatching since I was 12, so I was very keen to explore remote areas. But this was by far the most remote place I'd ever been to: about 1000 kilometers (621 mi.) from the North Pole and about 2000 kilometers (1242 mi.) from the nearest tree.

When I landed in early May, the temperature was still well below zero, but the days were already 24 hours long. The 24-hour light filled me with incredible energy. It was exciting to be in this unique place with only a dozen other people—people with character, like Tiny, the huge man with a big bushy beard who ran the station, and Leonard from Newfoundland who, with Tiny's help, built a dory that summer. There was also Carl, the other summer handyman. It was with Carl that I explored as much of the island as possible. Our first priority, every evening and every weekend, was to hike incredible distances and see as much Arctic life as possible. Together we covered a large part of the Fosheim Peninsula.

We had magical times watching muskoxen graze and their youngsters goof around on the tundra. We also saw Arctic wolves, sometimes two or three times a week. Once when we were working outside, we looked over our shoulders and saw a pack of six or seven wolves trotting along the ice, not even 300 meters (984 ft.) from

Eureka, Ellesmere Island, 79° North. I took this picture as I was arriving. Today Eureka is the second northernmost permanent community on Earth. The most northern permanent community is Alert, also on Ellesmere Island.

Leonard King and Tiny Powers built this dory the summer I was up at Eureka. Leonard would motor Carl and me across the fjord so we could hike on the opposite side of the weather station.

where we were standing. Where else in the world could you have wolves trot past as you work?

We were fortunate to be on the island during an Arctic hare population boom. During the late summer and fall big groups of these hares started to come together. Whole hillsides would be covered with up to 500 of them. A couple of times we were able to get close to them, especially when they started to amass.

We figured we would pull a "Farley Mowat" and simply pretend we were part of their group. We would get down on our knees and pretend to eat the vegetation, slowly working our way in, and it worked, but only the first few times. Once the wolves started to hunt them, the hares were more wary of us. We would watch huge numbers of hares on a faraway hillside suddenly take flight, followed closely by a couple of white dots—the wolves.

We also saw Peary's caribou, the rarest caribou in the world, at the northernmost point where they can be found. They survive in the most difficult terrain and weather conditions you could ever imagine. Over the past decade their numbers have been hard hit because of global warming. Warmer falls and springs mean that winter doesn't come overnight to the Arctic islands anymore.

SAY THE WORD!

Amass: to gather or heap together

High Arctic: the part of the Canadian Arctic that lies within the Arctic Circle

Peninsula: a piece of land almost surrounded by water, or projecting far into the sea or a lake

Peary's caribou are the smallest type of caribou in the Arctic because they live in such severe conditions and with fewer food options than their cousins, the barren ground caribou and woodland caribou.

It comes gradually now, with freezing sleet that the caribou cannot dig through. If a caribou can't paw through the snow to get to the vegetation beneath, it starves to death.

The first time we saw a caribou, we were climbing a local mountain. We stopped to rest and suddenly the snow patch next to us started to move, got up, and left. It was a caribou that had been lying on the snow to keep cool. They are so adapted to the cold that summer temperatures are uncomfortable for them.

Even when we weren't hiking, life at

Arctic wolves are bigger than their gray wolf cousins, often weighing over 45 kg (100 lb.). They have bigger hunting ranges than other wolves as well. Arctic wolves will prey on animals within a 1300–1600 kilometer (800–1000 mi.) square area.

Carl among Arctic hare. We would sneak up on them, pretending to be a part of their group. Arctic hare are huge, weighing up to 7 kilograms (15 lb.).

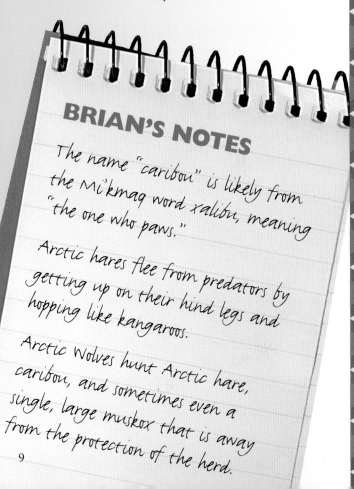

Muskox are called *omingmak* in Inupiaq, meaning "the animal with skin like a beard." They have changed little since the last ice age and their closest living relative is the takin, another goatlike animal that lives in the Himalayas.

the weather station was always interesting. The characters living in the North are often people who just don't like a complex city lifestyle. It's a simple life up there. I felt free. When you are in the North, day-to-day life doesn't include the same kinds of stress it does in the south: no major deadlines, no voicemail or email to answer. I can see how people are attracted to the northern lifestyle and never leave.

Living at Eureka allowed me to become a different person. When I came back from the North that fall I had a clear understanding of the direction I wanted my life to take and of what was important. Having walked so many kilometers where people may not have walked before was a real privilege.

I didn't really know a lot about the High Arctic when I arrived at the beginning of that summer. I remember going into the radio room at the station on my first night there and looking at a globe. I wanted to find Eureka and I found it just below that little metal disk that sits on the top of the globe. I realized I was sitting at the top of the world and it hit me like a ton of bricks. Since then I've sought out remote areas to

experience them as fully as possible. People say you go to places like Ellesmere Island to get away from it all, but I think you get to it all. It's where life really is.

BRIAN'S NOTES

The name "caribou" is likely from the Mi'kmaq word *xalibu*, meaning "the one who paws."

Arctic hares flee from predators by getting up on their hind legs and hopping like kangaroos.

Arctic Wolves hunt Arctic hare, caribou, and sometimes even a single, large muskox that is away from the protection of the herd.

9

THE CANARIES of the OCEAN

I've been all over the world whale-watching, but it was up in the Canadian Arctic where I had one of my most unique whale experiences.

A friend of mine, Pete, had built a tourist lodge at Cunningham Inlet on Somerset Island, Nunavut, just south of Cornwallis Island. He invited us to visit him there for a week. When we were there we did some fascinating hiking,

saw muskoxen, Peary's caribou, and a variety of birds. One of the most remarkable of the animals we saw was the beluga whale.

Cunningham Inlet is one of the few places in the world where belugas come to shed their skin every year. About 3000 whales arrive every July and travel up the shallow inlet lined with round pebbles to the Cunningham River estuary. When the fresh water flows over them,

The wriggling belugas in Cunningham Inlet. As adults, beluga whales are usually white, hence their name, which is Russian for "white one."

While hiking on Somerset Island we did some caving in an ice tunnel. There were some spectacular formations in the cave I am standing in here, much like stalactites, dripping from the cave ceiling.

the chemical makeup of their skin changes and it starts to come off in quarter-sized chunks. These belugas must feel like they are in whole-body scabs when they arrive at the inlet! In July the place is like a washing machine of thousands of whales, all wriggling and moving as if giving themselves full-body massages on the pebbles.

While watching them we had to tiptoe around the beach. The smallest noise could scare all the whales out of the inlet in the blink of an eye. Molting belugas scare easily and with good reason. When whales are that vulnerable and close to the shore, polar bears hunt them. Polar bears have been seen killing one beluga after another and hauling them out of the inlet.

We watched the whales from the top of a stepladder I had brought down from the lodge to get a good view of the inlet and all the belugas there. At times I would lie on my belly at

BRIAN'S NOTES

The beluga is the only whale that does a catastrophic molt. The whales lose and replace all of their skin in a matter of about 3 weeks.

Beluga whales can easily change their facial expressions because they have bulbous melons, pronounced lips, and the most mobile necks of any whale species.

There are about 70,000 beluga whales in the Arctic today, a healthy number.

surface level and look across, sometimes just 2 meters (6.5 ft.) away, at whales rubbing on the pebbles and behaving like jumping beans in the water. Their heads would sometimes come out of the water as they moved, giving me a chance to really look at their funny shaped foreheads, called melons. Belugas use their melons to communicate.

At the inlet I put a hydrophone in the water and listened to the whales squeaking and talking to each other. Beluga whales are called the canaries of the ocean. Their exquisite songs pulse from their melons, which actually change shape to direct sound or intensify sounds so

Pieces of beluga skin we found on the pebble beach of Cunningham Inlet. Sea birds and Arctic invertebrates like copepods and amphipods were feeding on the exfoliated skin all along the inlet.

they can echolocate, like a bat. Belugas use echolocation to communicate and to look for food and air holes when they are far beneath the Arctic ice. Just as we climb a hill to look for a good place to camp, scientists think belugas swim deep under the ice and send sound pulses up to find the air holes in the ice so they can breathe.

We were so enchanted by these whales that we really wanted to get closer to them in their environment. We knew we couldn't get any closer to the wriggling whales in the inlet, but we found out, through a local Inuit hunter, that there were a couple of dozen whales on the other side of the island. Along with another guest at the lodge, and with dry suits Pete lent us, we flew to the other side of Somerset. We thought it would be rude to go swimming right at the mouth of the creek where the whales were coming in.

Dee has climbed to the top rung to view and photograph the many belugas in the water below. We had to carry the ladder a few kilometers from Arctic Watch, the tourist lodge where we were staying.

While molting, belugas are very vulnerable to predators. They are also easy prey in the winter when they must work to keep air holes open. Sometimes a band of ice that is too broad and deep for them to escape under traps them. This entrapment is called a *sikujaumajut*.

It would be disturbing for them to suddenly see some big strangely dressed floating corks. With their sophisticated sonar, I figured they would come to us if we swam straight out to sea.

Polar bears eat seals and when you're dressed in a dry suit bobbing on the surface, you can look an awful lot like a seal. We had another friend stand on the shore with a shotgun to scare off any curious bears that might happen by. We got into our dry suits and jumped into the open ocean. We swam past icebergs and smaller chunks of ice until we were about a half kilometer (just over 1/4 mi.) away from the shore. We stopped and just bobbed like black corks on the surface. I snorkeled around for a while, freezing my lips and watching for whales. Little cold water invertebrates, such as copepods and amphipods, swam here and there. The water was crystal clear except at the surface, where it was blurry because the fresh water from the creek and melting ice were floating on top of the seawater.

Then, just like a ghost coming out of the darkness of the deep blue ocean, a beluga whale appeared right below me. He was swimming upside down with his head cocked, looking up at me. The beluga is the only whale with a neck this mobile. Several more whales came out of the deep blue until there were probably about a dozen. They were so white that there appeared to be a halo-like aura around their bodies. Curious, they came up closer and closer, and I could feel my body being pummeled by the sounds they were emitting. It was a supernatural, surreal, ghostly experience.

They came up as a group, had a look at us for about 25 seconds, and then they slipped away into the blue-black depths. It was one of the most satisfying and powerful natural history experiences of my life and will remain a vivid memory of grace and beauty.

SAY THE WORD!

Echolocation: the location of objects through reflected sound

Estuary: the tidal mouth of a river where the tide meets the stream

Invertebrate: an animal that does not have a back bone or spinal column

MUSKOX ISLAND

While I was working on Ellesmere Island I found the ultimate hiking path. It went from one side of the island to the other, straight through Ellesmere's herds of muskoxen. I couldn't hike the trail while I was there that summer, but I always dreamed of going back to traverse the island's only unglaciated pass.

Twenty years later, I found myself flying back to Ellesmere with a group of people who were just as excited as I was about hiking the pass. It turned out that "my route" included Sverdrup Pass, named after an explorer from Norway who hunted muskoxen there 100 years before.

We landed on the island at 2:00 AM. The sun was shining; it was a beautiful night. We were tired but supercharged by the midnight sun. We camped at a beautiful lake for a couple of nights before we started the trek.

At around 4:00 AM on the morning we were to begin the hike, Dee woke me up. "Brian, the tent is collapsing!" A huge storm had come in. The tent was closing in on my face. When it caved in, I got out and looked around. It looked as though my friends' tents had melted over them!

We spent the next day and night battling 80–100 kilometer per hour (50–62 mph) wind and rain, trying to hike. Snow buntings were being whipped around like bits of toilet paper. The wind was so powerful that when I relaxed my face and opened up my mouth, my cheeks billowed out. It was like I was eating huge jawbreakers! I dragged myself along with two hiking poles, walking in front of Dee, who walked in front of another hiker. We moved

The midnight sun lights up the Thorvald Peninsula on Ellesmere Island. When you are up in the Arctic during the summer months with the sun shining down at all hours, you feel like an Energizer bunny.

along just as Canada geese fly, with one cutting the wind and the others following.

We didn't get very far and soon gave up. The wind raged around us all night and the rain came down, leaking into our tents. When we woke up the next morning, the storm had moved off.

We hiked for several days through mostly clear skies, loving the weather and looking for muskoxen. We camped at the toes of glaciers, and we found muskox skeletons. We found one skeleton curled up at the toe of a steep glacier. We realized that one of the jawbones was broken and deduced that the muskox had died in pain. Maybe it was wandering in the pitch black of the 24-hour winter darkness, got disoriented, and slipped off the glacier.

After about a week of hiking, we arrived at Sverdrup Pass. It was a green meadow with babbling creeks, birds all over the place, and lots of vegetation. The pass was lush in comparison to everything we'd hiked through so far.

BRIAN'S NOTES

Peary's caribou is one of the most endangered and, after the Vancouver Island marmot, likely the most rare mammal in Canada. It is named for Robert E. Peary, who is said to have been the first to reach the North Pole in 1909.

Muskoxen use their massive heads to break the snow crust when it is too hard to paw through.

There are about 90,000 muskoxen in Canada today.

The muskox that wandered too far. This muskox was not brought down by wolves but fell from the glacier toe, broke its face, and died in pain. The fact is that animals make mistakes.

Otto and the Muskox

Otto Sverdrup was a Norwegian adventurer who explored the Canadian High Arctic from 1898 until 1902. Otto's expedition crossed the Sverdrup Pass on foot in the summer of 1899, marveling at the number of muskoxen. For these men, and many others before them, muskoxen were food. The Sverdrup expedition killed at least 200 muskoxen during the 4 years they were in the Arctic. Another famous Arctic explorer, Robert E. Peary, killed at least 800 muskoxen while he was exploring. The Canadian government made laws to prevent overhunting of muskoxen in 1917.

We camped there for several days and finally saw them, those crazy dust mops with legs. Muskoxen are Pleistocene relics. While the giant camels and giant beavers, the mastodons and mammoths died, the muskox survived. To look at them is like looking back in time.

We snuck up on them and watched them from distant ridges. We watched for long enough that we saw them goof around and play.

SAY THE WORD!

Glacier: a slow-moving mass of ice formed by a buildup of snow

Snow bunting: small white-and-black bird that lives on the Arctic tundra

Active layer: the layer of soil above frozen permafrost that freezes in the winter and thaws in the summer. It is always wet.

Muskoxen seem to have a sense of humor. In the summertime, when there is lots of food, they're buoyant and playful. The kids do goofy things, and the adults discipline them now and again. They're just the most un-oxenlike creatures you could ever watch!

We saw muskoxen everywhere—on the ridges, during late-night walks along muskox trails, and when we arose in the mornings. One day we watched a mother and her calf grazing, and soon after we came upon a group of nine

walking on. We also had to cross many an icy creek! After the plane came and picked us up, I realized that my dream hike had finally come true. Seeing the sweeping views of Ellesmere's mountains and hiking right across Canada's most northern island was amazing, and the crazy, windy start to the hike made the experience all the better!

When they feel threatened, muskoxen usually back into a defensive circle with their young in the center.

muskoxen. They felt a bit uneasy about us after a while and bunched up in a circle to defend themselves before heading out for greener pastures. Later we saw two rare Peary's caribou that ran away as soon as they saw us. We felt very lucky that day.

Dee and I collected some qiviut up on the pass, pulling it a bit at a time from the tundra. Qiviut, the underwool of the muskox, is one of the warmest fibers in the world. It helps to keep them warm and dry during the freezing winters.

We eventually made our way down from the pass to the other side of the island. We had a difficult, long descent down a steep boulder-strewn slope. The unstable conditions were made worse because of the active layer of permafrost just below the rocks we were

We would watch muskoxen rub against rocks and then steal in to collect the qiviut when they'd ambled away. We later had the qiviut spun into yarn and made into warm scarves.

The MINKE SERVED the ICE

Kayaking is one of the best ways to explore the rugged coastline of the Antarctic Continent. The glaciers spilling off the black cliffs make it difficult for large boats to land.

I feel like my first trip to the Antarctic actually started in Borneo when I was hiking there with Dee through the hottest jungles you can imagine. We were looking for the third great ape, the orangutan. Every evening I would read this book that I had picked up in the airport, *South*, by Ernest Shackleton, who explored the Antarctic 100 years ago. I would sit in my tent in the sweltering forests of Borneo reading about Shackleton's adventures in the ice. I did not yet know that 6 months later I would be in the Antarctic for the first time, seeing in abundance another of the world's great mammals: whales.

We sailed south from the tip of South America, through the often-stormy Drake's Passage. My first view of land was this island just off the northern tip of the Antarctic Continent. It came out of the mist, a white dog's tooth of fluted near-vertical ice slopes. It looked like some of the backdrops you see in science fiction movies. Soon after that we were looking at the continent.

These Adelie penguins are on a bergie bit, a large chunk of ice broken off of an iceberg. They watched us as our ship motored past. Our vantage point on the ship allowed us to watch the penguins rocket out of the water like bullets as they hopped onto the ice.

We sailed into the archipelago and I was stunned. The black basalt rock seemed to grow straight out of the ocean. The peaks had massive cornices that were laden with snow and ice, and every once in a while we would watch avalanches cascading off the peaks. We passed by icebergs, some of them crowded with penguins that stood watching the ship, their heads turning. The water was absolutely calm, like a mirror. And there were whales 360 degrees around us. We could identify minke and humpback whales, 2 of the 11 species we eventually identified.

BRIAN'S NOTES

The Antarctic Treaty was first signed by 12 nations in 1959. By 2005 there have been 45 nations that agree to its conditions, one of which is that the Antarctic Continent will only be occupied for peaceful scientific research and tourism.

Humpback whales gain about 10 tonnes (9.84 tn.) feeding on krill during the short Antarctic summer. They are mammalian tankers, converting the krill into fat and oil. People used whale oil to light lamps in Paris and London in the 1800s and early 1900s, and as an ingredient in fine oils and perfumes.

I've always been fascinated with whales, ever since I was a boy looking at the posters with the little human in the bottom left-hand corner and the big whales pictured above. But when you see whales on a poster you just can't relate to them in the same way you can when you see them in the wild, especially if the whales decide to approach you and make contact.

During that first trip to the Antarctic, the whales were aloof and distant. But over the last 4 years I've noticed (and expedition leaders confirm it) that the whales are changing: they're getting curious. For a couple of generations any human in the Antarctic was there to kill whales. It makes sense that a wild whale would be reluctant to come close to people. Now they are starting to get curious because more and more tourist ships are coming into Antarctic waters. Whales are big-brained animals, more than capable of curiosity, but it is hard to imagine how intelligent they are until you interact with them.

On my last couple of trips to the Antarctic, whales have approached us and done amazing things. On one trip a juvenile minke whale with a sense of humor came up to us. The whale came over to our Zodiac boat, then went to the other boats in the water. Now and again he would spy hop to have a better look. He would hop up so his head came out of the water until his eye was level with our boat or above it, then he would slide back into the water again. When he did this, we became excited. When you are whale-watching it's not like sitting at an African waterhole where you have to be absolutely quiet to see the life. When you're with whales, the more excited you get, the more excited they seem to get.

This minke whale started doing what seemed like silly things. It did barrel rolls. It showed its tail fluke and its pectoral fins,

then it started bringing ice chunks over to us. The whale would balance an ice chunk the size of a coffee can on its nose, bring it over, and drop it right in front of us, then disappear under the water. It would swim right under our boats then reappear on the other side, get another chunk of ice, and bring it over. It played with us for about an hour.

Another species of whale that has approached us in the Antarctic is the humpback whale. Humpbacks are big, barnacle-covered whales, measuring 10-plus meters (33 ft.). They are rorqual baleen whales, just like finback and minke whales, which means they have specialized feeding strategies that allow them to feed mostly on krill. When the humpbacks approached us, some of our friends were in kayaks in the water. I'll never forget the look on their faces when these whales came right up alongside them, sometimes rolling right over so we could see their beautiful white underbellies. They were like sychronized swimmers, weighing

Many Antarctic outposts like this one are used for important scientific study on anything from climate change to penguin behavior. Called "Bahia Paraiso," this station is surrounded by a large gentoo penguin colony.

Southern Right whales also inhabit the Southern Ocean, like this one that I photographed from my kayak. Both are baleen whales, and like humpbacks, the right whales are slowly recovering from near extinction due to whaling.

Sometimes the humpbacks we encountered made deep bellowing noises as they surfaced. Humpback whales produce a wide variety of sounds, including the lowest and highest possible frequencies a human can hear. They don't have vocal cords, but they use muscles in their respiratory tract to sing.

40 tonnes (39.3 tn.) apiece. Sometimes they would make deep bellowing noises as they surfaced. They seemed to be excited about our presence and about how excited we were to see them.

Being land animals, we don't really understand that much about whales. We only see them for brief glimpses when they come to the surface or if we're lucky enough to slip into the water and swim with them. When they display curiosity and goofiness in front of us we can begin to understand what they are, and understanding them leads to an appreciation and, ultimately, to conservation efforts. Making contact with the Antarctic whales has helped me, and many others, to argue for their preservation.

SURVIVING UNDER *the* MIDNIGHT SUN

While I was at Eureka I was able to watch some of the most amazing birds, which migrate to the High Arctic every summer. I also developed an interest in botany. I built myself a full-sized plant press and started thumbing through my guide to Arctic plants. I came to appreciate the microclimates within the expansive environment and gained first-hand experience with the indifferent severity of the Arctic climate.

My fellow handyman, Carl, and I were lucky to have met two botanists who were doing field studies on the island. They loaned us a dissecting microscope for the summer and were our source of inspiration. They lived about 30 kilometers (19 mi.) away from Eureka at Windy Lake. We hiked up to see them twice, bringing plants that we were stumped on, and they would help us.

The absolute beauty of these tiny plants and their ability to survive in the Arctic amazed me. We saw plants like the spider plant, which reproduces by sending tendrils out in a 5-centimeter (2 in.) circumference around it. A baby plant grows at the end of each tendril. There was another plant we loved called *Saxifraga tricuspidata*. The three-lobed leaves

Saxifraga tricuspidata turns a golden color in "flop," as Carl and I called fall. We would watch whole hillsides covered by this plant turn golden red and then flop over the course of a day or two.

This type of saxifrage plant was named "spider plant" by whalers and sailors because of its round body and long, leggy tendrils ending with daughter plants.

Red knots travel from South America to the Arctic every summer, risking starvation on their journey to build nests on the tundra, which may or may not be free of snow when they arrive.

on this plant would turn a golden color in the fall. But fall only lasted a couple of days, and nothing really "fell" anyway because all the plants are so short. For this reason, Carl and I called the season "flop" instead of fall. The seasons are so short in the Arctic that the plants really must make the most of the 24-hour light during the summer.

Sometimes—and more often now with global warming—the seasons in the Arctic don't come on schedule. When this happens, all life suffers. If the winter doesn't come overnight but arrives as freezing rain, the caribou can't paw through the ice to graze. And if winter lingers into spring, migrating birds, like the ruddy turnstone and the red knot, arrive on Ellesmere after their long migration from South America, Europe, and Africa to find nothing to eat.

When I arrived at Eureka that summer, I saw first-hand how a lingering winter can affect the ruddy turnstone, named for its funny behavior of turning stones to find food. Most of these birds winter in Europe but have been found as far south as Africa. They migrate to Ellesmere Island every spring. Like red knots, another bird that summers on the island, ruddy turnstones change the sizes of their organs and muscles when they prepare to fly to the Arctic. The adjustments their bodies make for migration depends upon the food they can find at the stopover areas on the way to Ellesmere, but it is also important for the birds to find food when they arrive on the island. That summer there was no food for the ruddy turnstones when they arrived, just snow and ice, so most of them died. I found their bodies everywhere. I actually packaged several up and sent them to a university down south. Researchers who performed the autopsies on the bird's bodies found that their stomachs were completely empty. These birds had trusted their instincts and had flown a great distance to where a summer food supply had always been found. That year, the food simply wasn't there.

When migration fails, the Arctic food chain has to adjust. Arctic foxes prey on migratory birds like jaegers, but to survive they must also depend on lemmings, which reach peak numbers about every four years. From plants to birds to rodents to predators, the timely turning of the seasons makes the difference between life and death. People living in the Arctic, of course, also must cope with the harsh climate.

It was through personal experience that I gained an even greater appreciation for how Arctic plants and animals survive. Carl and I hiked through a blizzard one morning on the way home from visiting our botanist friends. It was late August. We had spent the evening visiting and started hiking back to Eureka at 6:00 AM to be back for dinner. A serious storm set in, with horizontal sleet blowing at us all the

Lemmings build simple burrows in the tundra in the summer and a similar network of tunnels in the snow during the winter.

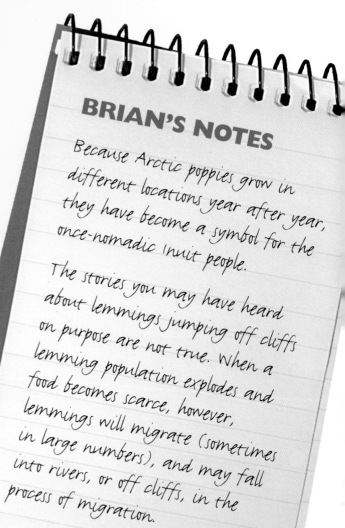

BRIAN'S NOTES

Because Arctic poppies grow in different locations year after year, they have become a symbol for the once-nomadic Inuit people.

The stories you may have heard about lemmings jumping off cliffs on purpose are not true. When a lemming population explodes and food becomes scarce, however, lemmings will migrate (sometimes in large numbers), and may fall into rivers, or off cliffs, in the process of migration.

Bug Jacuzzis

Many Arctic plants produce heat instead of nectar. Flowers such as the Arctic poppy are parabolic, and they follow the sun around as it goes through the sky. The insides of the bowl-shaped flowers are usually a few degrees warmer than the surrounding air. Arctic plants don't rely solely on insects for pollination simply because there aren't many insects up there. Still, when a tiny insect comes along in the cool air needing to warm up, they see these bowl-shaped flowers and climb into their own little private Jacuzzis. They warm up and then they fly off again, thereby pollinating a plant.

The Arctic poppy has a bowl-shaped flower that always faces the midnight sun.

way home. The rain was pushing right through our coats, and we developed a level of hypothermia that came very close to killing us both. After stumbling numbly for hours through the sleet, tripping over hummocks the size of basketballs, we finally reached Eureka, miserably cold. Carl was sick for about a week after that, and I was exhausted for days. The day after our brush with death everything was frozen solid. Winter had arrived.

I'll never forget the flock of eider ducks on a little pond we came across during our walk through the sleet. They were young and couldn't yet fly. We stood on the edge of this 2-meter (6.5 ft.) pond and the eiders swam nervously in circles. I always wondered if they made it through the storm. Everything operates on such a tight schedule up there. Both plants and animals must either adapt or die. There is no forgiveness in the High Arctic.

King eider ducks, like this female, eat aquatic animals like mollusks, found on the ocean floor. They are fantastic divers. One record has a king eider feeding in water 55 meters (180 ft.) deep.

KINGS *in* THEIR FINEST SUITS

When people think about the Antarctic, they think about penguins. There are 17 species of penguins in the world but only 4 of those nest on the Antarctic Continent. Most of them nest in the sub-Antarctic islands, the most famous of which is South Georgia Island, where the king penguins have their great colonies.

When Dee and I joined an expedition to see the king penguins of South Georgia, we almost didn't get to see them. The day we found a big colony, I headed out with the rest of the staff in the Zodiac boat to check out the beach. We had a hard time getting ashore because a catabatic wind was starting to blow. When we finally landed on the beach, it felt like we were in the middle of a cyclone. The wind was whipping sand at us with such ferocity that it was stinging my face. Even the penguins were being thrown off balance. We had to get back into the Zodiac only 5 minutes after landing. It was ripping my heart out to leave the penguins so soon, but we had to, or risk being trapped there overnight.

We went back to the ship and tried to find another colony in a more sheltered location. We tried all day without success. Finally the winds picked up to about 75 knots, which is about 150 kilometers per hour (93 mph). The whole ship was listing onto its side. When I walked down the hall, it was like I was in a carnival crooked house where everything is on an angle. We sought refuge in a steep, deep fjord where the cliffs protected us from the winds. There we waited out the storm.

By the time we headed out of the mouth of the fjord, night had fallen and it was dark.

Winds sweeping off the tops of South Georgia Island's glaciers whipped the ocean into a fury when we tried to land at a king penguin colony.

The largest king penguin colonies can include as many as 60,000 pairs and their chicks. They prefer to be close to each other, but they also guard their own territory vigorously, protecting their eggs.

We launched the Zodiac boats into the water with a crane on board the mother ship. Driving a Zodiac through ice can be tricky.

We only had one more day to pull off a landing at a king penguin colony before we had to move on to the Antarctic Continent. After a crazy, sleepless night of listening to the wind, talking to the expedition leader, and even shining a floodlight on a beach to see how big the waves were, we decided the weather looked good enough for us to attempt a landing.

In the predawn light we dropped a Zodiac and headed for the shore. It was magical being on the beach before the sun came above the horizon. I watched the colors of the sky change over a multitude of king penguins. All along the beach were thousands of penguins, and beyond the beach, up the hill, rose a colony of penguins, numbering at least 55,000 pairs. Including all the nonbreeding and young birds, there were probably about 200,000 penguins.

King penguins are colorful. They have beautiful black faces, black eyes, and a teardrop shape of orange and yellow that

At any time during the year there are king penguin chicks of various ages in the Antarctic colonies, which stretch from barren beaches to grassy tussocks—anywhere at sea level that is free of ice and snow.

starts beside their eyes and extends down their necks to their chests. Their faces remind me of the candy corn I used to get as a kid at Halloween. It was overwhelming to see them all in their finest black-and-white suits, standing around, each of them about a meter (3.3 ft.) tall.

I had a chest-high dry suit on, so I stayed at the beach and set my tripod up in the water. I filmed penguins all around me as they were coming in. As I stood in the water up to my waist filming them, penguins were darting around me, washing up with the surf, and then waddling up to join the others on the beach. Finally I decided to go inland and I found Dee sitting in the colony with a crowd

of penguins. The best way to penguin-watch is to sit and wait for them to come to you. She had penguins all around her. There was a penguin nibbling on her boot and a few standing close and looking at her. Beyond her, the great volume of king penguins stretched all the way up the slope.

The masses of penguins reminded me of the groupings of people I have seen at a rock concert! There were small pockets of fuzzy chicks, adults looking in all directions, and others making their way through the crowds. Occasional brawls broke out, with flippers flapping and penguins racing after each other.

Mating For Life

When you see a boy and a girl holding hands, they are expressing their appreciation for one another. In biological terms they are pair bonding, which is the way animals establish relationships. Most penguins mate for life. When a pair reunites after being apart from each other, they also pair bond. Chinstrap and Adelie penguins, which nest on the Antarctic Continent, "hold hands" by sticking their beaks up into the sky, putting their little wings out, and pumping their bodies full of air to let out a funny croaking sound called an ecstasy call. King penguins solidify their relationships with their mates by head bowing, a very formal greeting.

The penguins would wash up to the colony in groups of 30–50, sometimes catapulting right out of the water onto the beach. Then they made their way to the teeming throngs on the beach and above.

Sometimes innocent bystanders caught a flipper in the face during these altercations! And we could see some of the adults bowing to each other, pair bonding. Eventually the winds picked up again and we had to get back to the ship. It was hard to leave.

King penguins, gulls, and seals away from the main king colony near an old whaling station. Nonbreeding king penguins stay far away from the breeding colony, hunting for food.

Sometimes while we were kayaking along the coast of Ellesmere Island we encountered huge icebergs. We paddled past this one in Hayes Fjord.

When we went ashore we found evidence of Thule communities, ancient groups of Inuit people. This snow knife probably hadn't been removed from its spot for 500 years. I put the knife back where I found it.

TUSKS and PAWS and UNICORNS

There is something magical about kayaking. Being so low to the water gives you an incredible feeling of being at one with the ocean. We used foldable kayaks when we set out to explore the east coast of Ellesmere Island because they were easiest to stuff into the Twin Otter plane that took us there.

When we arrived, we found that one of the fjords we were paddling was almost ice free. The water there probably hadn't been open for centuries. The last people to paddle up the fjord were likely the Inuit who lived

Icebergs calve, or break off, from glaciers like this one spilling into the water off Ellesmere Island.

there 500 or 600 years ago. Whenever we found a good landing and went ashore, we always came across evidence of an ancient Inuit community. Paddling the same waters as they once did was very exciting. We felt like we were pioneers.

We were glad to be in kayaks because the rugged coastline was virtually impossible to explore on foot. So many of the glaciers come cascading off the steep mountain slopes and calve icebergs as big as houses right into the ocean. At times I felt as if I were paddling within a cathedral of ice. During this amazing kayaking journey I saw walruses and narwhal for the first time in my life, as well as a curious polar bear.

We saw probably 200 walrus during our 2-week trip, and we always wanted to get close to them. But there is nothing worse in a walrus's mind than to have the Starship Enterprise members suddenly materialize right in front of them. When we did approach, we always paddled up slowly and only when we knew they were aware of us.

Getting close to them was a profound experience. They look like aliens. When they blink, their eyes seem to disappear down into their skulls, and when they open them again their bloodshot eyes pop out like golf balls. The blood vessels in their eyes increase in size to help them cool off. Walruses also have blood vessels on the surface of their fins that

SAY THE WORD!

Calve: to shed a mass of ice; an iceberg can also be called a calf

Pinniped: any aquatic mammal with limbs ending in fins

Carnivore: a mammal with powerful jaws and teeth adapted for stabbing, tearing, and eating flesh

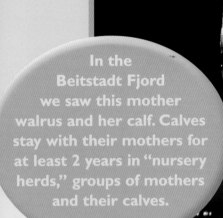

In the Beitstadt Fjord we saw this mother walrus and her calf. Calves stay with their mothers for at least 2 years in "nursery herds," groups of mothers and their calves.

allow them to get rid of excess heat. Walruses are pinnipeds, like seals and sea lions, but they are unique. They are surely one of the weirdest creatures on the planet.

One day we came across a mother walrus and her baby sunning themselves on a beautiful chunk of ice. The baby, with no tusks, looked like a deep-sea oceanic worm covered in wrinkles. It was nursing as we approached them, drinking milk that is the consistency of toothpaste that the mom squirts into the baby's mouth.

Another day, just as we were paddling away from a group of walruses, we noticed a polar bear watching us from the shore. The bear was a long way away, at least a kilometer (0.62 mi.), so we felt pretty safe. We excitedly watched him with our binoculars. As soon as the bear figured out that we were looking at him, he stood up on his hind legs and looked at us. But when it became obvious to the bear that we were all looking at him, he became

BRIAN'S NOTES

Walrus milk is about 30 percent fat. Because of the fatty diet, a walrus calf grows about 10 to 15 cm (4–6 in.) each month and gains 0.7 to 0.9 kilograms (1.5–2 lb.) per day.

Narwhal tusks were once believed to come from unicorns (the hunters who sold the tusks never told anyone otherwise). Some kings believed that no harm would come to them if they drank from "unicorn horn" goblets.

wary and jumped into the water and swam away. Seeing a polar bear this far north is rare, so we felt very privileged to have seen him.

Almost every night I camped by myself in my sleeping bag without a tent. Many nights I set up my sleeping bag about a half meter (1.65 ft.) away from the water. Sometimes I would wake to the sound of a walrus blowing air out of his nostrils. Another time I saw a ringed seal floating on his back with his nostrils above the water, moving his head back and forth. This way he didn't have to hold his breath as he searched for food. Several times I would hear narwhal, the whale known as the unicorn of the sea.

We saw narwhal during the day as well. One curious narwhal youngster, still without its tusk, came over and spent about a half hour with us, surfacing and diving, but most of the narwhal kept their distance. With my binoculars, I saw them jousting above the surface, clicking their big tusks together. Narwhal live in the most remote of our Arctic

waters. To see the narwhal, the weird-looking walruses, and the polar bear was very special.

At the end of the incredible journey we paddled up a fjord, landed, and set to work moving enough rocks out of the way at the toe of a glacier to allow an airplane to land. It was a great feeling to watch the plane touch down on the strip that we had made.

The Twin Otter plane landing on our makeshift airstrip. While he appreciated our effort, the pilot said we would never land in that spot again!

Walruses are very gregarious animals. They congregate by the hundreds in huge groups, one word for which in Inuit means "an ugly." Walruses are rarely out on the ice or land alone.

LIVING on the EDGE

On my second expedition to the Antarctic we really wanted to cross the Antarctic Circle. When we were just within a kilometer (0.62 mi.) of it, though, an ocean of pack ice blocked us. Pack ice is broken fast ice that has been churned up by the ocean. Fast ice is the kind of ice you can skate on. Simply plowing through this ice is dangerous because huge chunks of pack ice can stop ships, bogging them down. In 1915, the English explorer Ernest Shackleton was caught in pack ice that quickly turned into fast ice. He was stuck for 10 months until frost heaves came through his ship and crushed it like a house of cards. The ship sank as the men stood on the ice and watched.

It was easy to understand why the captain of our ice-reinforced ship did not want to go very far into the pack ice! We followed along its edge until we could find a spot where we could dip in far enough to pass into the circle. A few people on the boat had global positioning system (GPS) receivers so we knew exactly when we were there. When we were at the circle, we celebrated while looking at huge icebergs lined up in the near distance. Lying out on the ice pancakes close by were dozens of crabeater seals accompanied by giant petrels and Antarctic skuas. With the birds, seals, and

Negotiating brash ice, small floating bits of ice, in the Lemaire Channel between the Antarctic Peninsula and Booth Island. After we discovered we wouldn't be able to get through the channel, we dropped our Zodiacs and went for a spin through the ice.

Celebrating our crossing of the Antarctic Circle on the deck. We almost didn't make it because of the pack ice.

icebergs, we had perfect company for an Antarctic Circle visit!

The summer Antarctic sun is warm enough to melt pack ice pretty quickly. When the ice melts it releases algae, which is growing on the underside of the ice. As that algae breaks free of the ice, it provides nutrients for krill, the zooplankton that is the basic building block of Antarctic ecology. Penguins, seals, whales, and many other Antarctic creatures feed on krill. As we cruised along the melting pack-ice edge we saw seabirds, such as giant petrels, seals hauled up on the ice, and several whales. All of these animals live on or near the edge—the ice edge—where they can either feed on krill or on other animals that feed on krill.

After we had reached the Antarctic Circle, the captain turned the ship around. We wanted to make a shore landing and camp out on one of the islands in the Antarctic Peninsula. We wanted to see what it felt like to live on the edge. We motored through the night to our destination. When it got light enough to see,

Crabeater seals hang out on pack ice and actually eat krill, not crabs. They interlock their top and bottom jaw to create a sieve in order to strain krill from seawater, much like baleen. In fact, the amount of krill that crabeater seals eat every year is more than that eaten by all the Antarctic baleen whales.

into the ocean, a pod of eight orcas sliced through the water nearby and even approached us. Killer whales also frequent the ice edge to prey on seals.

In a couple of days we found a place to land. We got ready to camp, reviewing the rules of the Antarctic Treaty: bring no food and bring back all waste. Dee and I chose not to use a tent because we knew that sleeping out in the open would be the best way to experience the Antarctic night. With three Weddell seals looking on, we set up camp near the water.

Weddell seals prefer to haul themselves up on fast ice, or on the shore, unlike their crabeater cousins. They eat fish that eat krill, hunting them by stealth. Video footage from cameras attached to Weddell seals show them coming within centimeters of fish without startling

we were between Booth Island and the Antarctic Peninsula in the Lemaire Channel. This is a very famous channel because it's very narrow, with vertical rock walls on both sides and many bulging glaciers. When we entered the channel it was chock full of pack ice but the captain pushed on, hoping we could get past it. I hung over the bow to watch the ice break. In the end, we met with ice too thick to plow through and many icebergs. We had to retreat, following the trail we had carved through the ice.

On the way to a better landing spot we sighted humpback whales, so we got into our Zodiac boats and were able to get close to them. While the Zodiacs were being craned

BRIAN'S NOTES

The killer whales we saw outside the Lemaire Channel had eye patches that were more yellow than the ones on the orcas in our northern waters. Some scientists suspect these Antarctic orcas may be a different sub species.

Sheathbills are the only land bird in the Antarctic.

Weddell seals, named for the British explorer James Weddell, live farther south than any other mammal.

A gentoo penguin defending its nest from a sheathbill. Sheathbills spend most of their time scavenging in penguin colonies.

them. They also blow air into ice crevices to flush out fish.

After we tucked in for the night I watched a skua, the vulture of the Antarctic, touring the camp looking for opportunities. As I was lying quietly I could hear a distant colony of penguins, the funny whimpering of the Weddell seals off in the distance, and every now and then a group of raucous trilling terns interrupted everything. Sometimes I could hear the sound of a whale blowing in the distance and I would turn over, look into the fjord, and see the whale or penguins on the beach.

Dee told me that in the middle of the night a sheathbill landed on her chest. When she wiggled her eye over to look out of the breathing hole she'd made by pulling the drawstring on her sleeping bag, she was looking up at this crazy bird that was bobbing its head and looking down at her eyeball. Sheathbills look like chickens with a serious case of acne. They are the cleanup detail of the Antarctic, eating the lumpy bits out of penguin poop, the afterbirth from seals, and spilt krill. If they get half a chance, they will steal and eat penguin eggs. For a silly, brief moment,

Dee wondered if eyeballs were on the menu!

Before we left our campsite the next morning, I went down to the water and filmed the sunrise spangles of light that were dancing on the surface and shining through the water droplets melting off icicles. The droplets were like diamonds falling into the water. In the middle of all this beauty, a penguin popped up, star spangles all around its silhouette. It was one of those tiny moments that make you realize the value of life and living, and the importance of seeking out the wilderness.

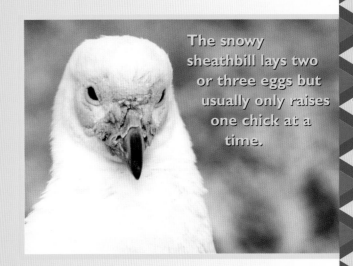

The snowy sheathbill lays two or three eggs but usually only raises one chick at a time.

SUPERBEARS
of the NORTH

Every Arctic researcher, scientist, or worker has a horror story to tell about being stalked by a polar bear, a close call, or about a friend who was taken by one. The polar bear is the ultimate animal, the ultimate carnivore, the ultimate owner of the land. It is a "superbear," living in the most ridiculous conditions, where it gets dark for at least 4 months of the year, the temperatures plunge to -60°C (-76°F), and the winds blow for weeks on end. I have seen polar bears in the wild a few times, but one trip allowed me to see them as few people do.

That summer was the worst ice year that the Canadian Arctic had seen in 20 years. An icebreaker from the Canadian Coast Guard had to break a trail for us out of Frobisher Bay near Iqaluit, Nunavut. I was ecstatic about the ice because it creates an edge situation where wildlife gathers—a place to see seals, whales, walrus, and polar bears. Because of the ice, we saw 26 polar bears on the trip.

Our first sighting of a polar bear was the best. We left Iqaluit in the afternoon, following the icebreaker, and by the next morning we were on the other side of the pack ice following the ice edge slowly northward. We spent some time on the deck, looking through our binoculars. Sure enough, we came across a polar bear. He didn't seem

Even though the ice caused some problems for our boat leaving Iqaluit, we were more than pleased. Because of the heavy ice in the Arctic that summer, we saw more polar bears in the wild than ever before.

worried about us, so we decided to drop the Zodiacs in the water to get a closer look. Carefully, we brought our Zodiacs up onto the ice and watched the polar bear from a distance. It was one of the most amazing sights.

We watched him with our binoculars jumping between ice floes, splashing into the water and then climbing out again. The bear was huge, probably about 680 kilograms (1500 lb.). Polar bears are the biggest bears in the world but this bear was so graceful in the

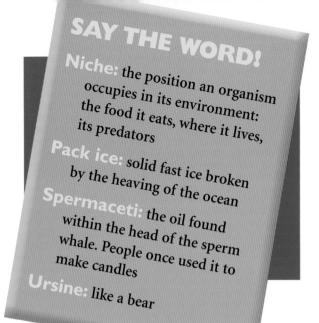

Polar bears are the largest land carnivore. The largest polar bear recorded was a male who weighed 1002 kilograms (2209 lb.) and measured 3.7 meters (12 ft.)!

While walruses often sleep on the ice, they can also sleep in the water. They have special sacs under their throats that they can fill with air to keep them afloat while they rest.

water he was like an ursine Olympic swimmer coming out of the pool. When he came out he would shake or roll on the snow to squeeze the water out of his fur. We just sat there and watched this bear totally at ease in his marine environment, many kilometers from land.

The joy of it all was that the bear didn't care that we were there. He would sometimes walk toward us, stand up and sniff, and try to figure out what we were. But then he went back to doing what polar bears do on the ice: hang out, look around, go for a swim, come back out, shake, roll, and continue on with life. It was hard to pull away from watching him, but after about 45 minutes we headed back to the ship and continued on our journey.

Still in Canadian waters, out in the open ocean, we came across a sperm whale at the surface doing its deep-breathing exercises before diving. After they fill their lungs with oxygen, sperm whales dive down a vertical kilometer (0.62 mi.), where some scientists think they sit in the inky depths and hunt giant squid. Sperm whales have big square heads that are full of spermaceti oil, used for

A polar bear's sense of smell is very acute, and is its most important sense for detecting prey on land. A polar bear can smell a seal more than 32 kilometers (20 mi.) away.

intensifying these sound blasts. Heating or cooling this specialized oil may also help them perform their deep dives.

When we were back near the pack ice we were in polar bear territory again. It seemed there were polar bears wherever we went. In one area we found eight polar bears. Three of these were a mother and two cubs. Polar bear moms stick very close to their young, and we had the opportunity to watch her trotting away, hustling her babies along, always stopping to make sure they caught up to her. A big male polar bear will kill a cub if it has a chance.

We were in Lancaster Sound, the perfect place to see these bears because it is a polynya, an area of permanently open water, even in winter, where life congregates. It's a place of plenty, full of food. The amount of life we saw was staggering.

At Bylot Island we saw vast numbers of thick-billed murres, little auks that eat fish, krill, and other zooplankton, filling the same niche that penguins fill at the South Pole. We also saw several narwhal, and in one

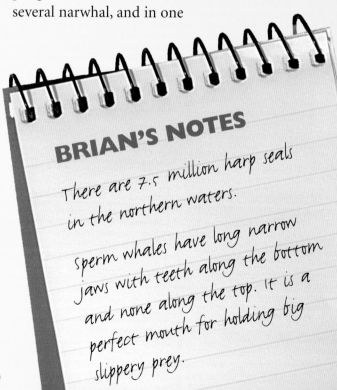

BRIAN'S NOTES

There are 7.5 million harp seals in the northern waters.

Sperm whales have long narrow jaws with teeth along the bottom and none along the top. It is a perfect mouth for holding big slippery prey.

A polar bear's fur is not white; it is transparent with a hollow core. The fur only seems white because the hollow cores scatter and reflect visible light. In 1979, three polar bears at the San Diego Zoo turned green because there was a harmless algae growing in the cores of their fur! A salt solution took care of the algae, restoring the bears' "white" fur.

Thick-billed murres nest in huge Arctic colonies on narrow cliff ledges. Some of these murres also nest off the coasts of Labrador and Newfoundland.

the winter when the seals have to carve holes in the ice to get air. It is much easier for the bears to hunt in the winter than in the summer, although it requires incredible patience. Polar bears will sit for hours, even days, around seal holes. Then, in the blink of an eye, they force their pie-plate-sized paw through the ice over the breathing hole and pull a seal out through the hole. Polar bears are so powerful they have even been seen hauling beluga whales, which weigh between 408 and 635 kilograms (900–1400 lb.), out of the water.

This was my seventh trip to the Arctic, and I've never seen so many polar bears. We were meeting bears that may never have encountered people before. Many of these kings of the north were still behaving as they should, as the owners of the land, sea, and ice.

of the fjords of Bylot Island we watched the ocean boil with harp seals for about 4 hours one evening. We guessed we saw about 20,000 of them that night. They are beautiful seals with black faces and a black double crescent that looks like a harp on their backs.

Polar bears feast on these and other seals in

WANDERING SOUTH

E ver since I started birdwatching when I was 12, I always dreamed about South Georgia Island in the Antarctic. I had seen so many pictures in *National Geographic* of its huge colonies of amazing sea birds and king penguins, not to mention the other animals living in the Southern Ocean that surrounds it: whales, sea lions, and seals. Because it is so remote, I never thought I would get there, but now I have—twice.

The typical first view of South Georgia is out of this world. The sharp peaks of the first set of islands appear out of the mist. High cliffs and rock walls are draped with dark

South Georgia Island always seems to appear out of a mist. Its steep and rugged coastline makes it inhospitable to humans, but it is home to a great number of amazing species, like the albatross.

clouds, and all of the valleys have huge glaciers billowing out of them. Another thing you notice right away is how the surrounding ocean modifies the weather. Because of moderate winds, you can actually find lush grasses and thick mats of moss growing on South Georgia Island. And the winds that South Georgia is known for are also important to the great sea birds that nest on the island, particularly the albatross.

SAY THE WORD!

Tube-nose: a family of seabirds, including albatross, shearwaters, and petrels. These birds get rid of the salt from the seawater they drink by dripping it from their tube-noses.

Radio telemetry: used by biologists to study animal movements. Radio transmitters are attached to the animals that give off silent signals that can be received by biologists using a special antenna that shows where the animal is.

Primary feather: one of the main flight feathers projecting along the outer edge of a bird's wing

Albatross define flight. They are the most magnificent birds on the open ocean. Evolutionary biologists think that albatross evolved in the Southern Ocean to utilize the powerful winds that it generates. It is the most violent ocean on the planet. While many sailors have gone down in its huge wind-whipped waves, the albatross requires the ocean and its strong winds to survive.

When the winds drop below 18 kilometers per hour (11 mph), albatross settle like ducks onto the ocean. They need the winds to stay aloft because they are so big. With a wingspan of over 3 meters (10 ft.), albatross need a runway to take off. Some of them use a cliff to launch themselves. Then, grabbing a wave of wind and with a little leap, they're up in the air like Superman. They fly holding out their long, narrow wings, designed to keep them aloft for long distances. Radio telemetry bands attached to albatross have proven that they can fly up to 15,000 kilometers (9321 mi.) on one food-gathering expedition. It may take them 2 weeks to gather food for their young, riding on the powerful winds of the Southern Ocean.

I always thought the open ocean would be a lonely place, but the Southern Ocean is alive. Every time I went out on deck and looked, I saw birds. There were always Wilson's storm petrels, tube-noses like the albatross but much smaller, dancing out there on the surface. Behind the ship, there would always be one or two albatross, sometimes a dozen. In one 4-hour period I saw five species of albatross, sometimes flying so close I could see them looking at me. Many had exquisite markings on their beaks and heads.

On one trip south I was lucky enough to pay a visit to Albatross Island, near South Georgia. When we landed we walked past a large group of seals in the tussocks until we came across nesting albatross. We continued walking until we arrived at a place where there were many albatross, and some of them were dancing. The males spread their wings,

cock their heads high, and clack their beaks as they dance about. The females check out the males and the males check out the females. They mate for life and reinforce their relationship after their long forays out into the ocean with ritualistic dancing and head bobbing behavior.

There is nothing quite as magical as standing amidst the dancing albatross and hearing the wind slice through their wings as other albatross fly overhead. You can actually hear the wind screaming through their primary feathers as they fly and play and dance in the dynamic wind waves that are coming up over the ridge. It is such a privilege to be in a place where the albatross dance and nest and raise their young.

This grey-headed albatross is gliding on the crest of a wave of air. The winds generated by the Southern Ocean can take albatross on gliding, food-gathering adventures all the way around the Antarctic Continent.

An Antarctic fur seal in the tussocks on South Georgia Island. Our mother ship is anchored in the distance. We hiked through these tussocks to find the nesting albatross.

When albatross dance, it is like magic. The males move slowly, showing off for the females. It can take 1 or 2 years for an albatross to select a mate.

Saving the Albatross

The number of albatross roaming the Southern Ocean has been dropping for decades, mostly because of the long-line fishery. Long-line fishing boats may put out as much as 40 kilometers (25 mi.) of fishing line with 40,000 baited hooks. When the line is thrown off the back of the ship in the middle of the day, the following albatross see the bait and go after it, drowning in the process. The lines of hooks kill these birds that otherwise would live more than 60 years. Some albatross, such as the black-browed albatross, have dwindled to 50 percent of their numbers since the early 1950s. In order to help the albatross, researchers have been figuring out what they do and where they go, using radio telemetry to track them. Other researchers are working with fishers to limit the time of year and time of day they are fishing. If they put out hooks at night, for example, no albatross will be following to take the bait. There are also ways to redesign fishing boats so no sea bird has the opportunity to grab baited hooks. It is possible to fix the problem, but only with hard work and a lot of people working together. If the albatross disappear, the Southern Ocean will be a boring place, like the Serengeti without its wildebeest.

CONSERVATION—IT'S UP TO YOU!

If you'd like to learn more about or become involved in wildlife conservation, contact any or all of the following organizations.

Agreement on the Conservation of Albatrosses and Petrels
ACAP Interim Secretariat, Barry Baker
Australian Antarctic Division
Channel Highway, Kingston 7050
Tasmania, Australia
barry.baker@aad.gov.au +61 3 6232 3407
www.acap.aq

Antarctic and Southern Ocean Coalition
The Antarctica Project
1630 Connecticut Ave., NW Third Floor
Washington, D.C. 20009
202-234-2480 www.asoc.org

Calgary Zoo
1300 Zoo Road, SE
Calgary, AB T2E 7V6
403-232-9333 www.calgaryzoo.ab.ca

Canadian Nature Federation
1 Nicholas Street, Suite 606
Ottawa, Ontario K1N 7B7
cnf@cnf.ca 613-562-3447
www.cnf.ca

Canadian Parks and Wilderness Society
National Office
880 Wellington Street, Suite 506
Ottawa, Ontario K1R 6K7
info@cpaws.org 1-800-333-WILD
www.cpaws.org

Canadian Wildlife Federation
350 Michael Cowpland Drive
Kanata, Ontario K2M 2W1
info@cwf-fcf.org 1-800-563-WILD
www.cwf-fcf.org

Conservation of Arctic Flora and Fauna
Hafnarstraeti 97
600 Akureyri, Iceland
caff@caff.is www.caff.is

David Suzuki Foundation
2211 West 4th Avenue, Suite 219
Vancouver, BC V6K 4S2
solutions@davidsuzuki.org 1-800-453-1533
www.davidsuzuki.org

Ducks Unlimited (Wetland Conservation)
Box 1160
Oak Hammock Marsh, Manitoba R0C 2Z0
1-800-665-3835 www.ducks.ca

International Polar Heritage Committee
President - Susan Barr
Riksantikvaren - Directorate for Cultural Heritage
PO Box 8196 Dep
N-0034 Oslo, Norway
susan.barr@ra.no +47 - 22 94 04 00
www.polarheritage.com

The Jane Goodall Institute (Canada)
Mr. Nicolas Billon, Executive Assistant
P. O. Box 477, Victoria Station
Westmount, Quebec H3Z 2Y6
nicolas@janegoodall.ca 514-369-3384 (fax)
www.janegoodall.ca

Marmot Recovery Foundation
Marmot
Box 2332, Station A
Nanaimo, BC V9R 6X9
1-877-4MARMOT www.marmots.org

Polar Bears International
PO Box 66142
Baton Rouge, LA, USA 70896
225-923-3114 www.polarbearsalive.org

WWF Arctic Programme
Kristian Augusts gate 7A
Box 6784 St. Olavs Pl
N-0130 Oslo, Norway
arctic@wwf.no + 47 22 03 65 00
www.panda.org/arctic

Cool Sites on the Web:
Species At Risk: www.speciesatrisk.ca
Space for Species: www.spaceforspecies.ca
Hudson Bay Project:
    http://research.amnh.org/~rfr/hbp/main.html

When an Arctic hare is bouncing away from a predator, it can reach speeds up to 50 kilometers (31 mi.) per hour. Arctic hares are able to survive in the extremely dry climate of the polar desert. To find out more about the world's deserts and the animals that live in them, watch for my next book, *Amazing Animal Adventures in the Desert*.

INDEX

A free Teacher's Guide is available for this book at: http://www.fitzhenry.ca/guides.htm or call 1-800-387-9776.

Cover and interior design by John Luckhurst
All photographs by Brian and Dee Keating, except cover (polar bear) John Perret; 33 (walruses), 38–39 (polar bear), 40 (polar bear), 41 (thick-billed murres), back cover (walruses) by Image Matters/Graham Charles; 41 (polar bear and cubs) and 46–47 (Arctic hare) by John Gillespie

Edited by Meaghan Craven
Copyedited by Joan Tetrault
Proofread by Lesley Reynolds
Scans by St. Solo Computer Graphics

The publisher gratefully acknowledges the support of The Canada Council for the Arts and the Department of Canadian Heritage

THE CANADA COUNCIL | LE CONSEIL DES ARTS
FOR THE ARTS | DU CANADA
SINCE 1957 | DEPUIS 1957

We acknowledge the financial support of the Government of Canada through the Book Publishing Industry Development Program for our publishing activities.

05 06 07 08 09 / 5 4 3 2 1

First published in the United States in 2005 by
Fitzhenry & Whiteside
121 Harvard Avenue, Suite 2
Allston, MA 02134

National Library of Canada Cataloguing in Publication Data

Keating, Brian, 1955-
Amazing animal adventures at the poles / with Brian Keating.

(Going wild)
Includes index.
ISBN 1-894856-53-8 (bound).—ISBN 1-894856-54-6 (pbk.)

1. Animals—Polar regions—Juvenile literature. I. Title. II. Series:
Keating, Brian, 1955- . Going wild.

QL104.K42 2005   j591.7586
C2004-906730-3

Free teacher's guide available at www.fitzhenry.ca/guides or call 1-800-387-9776

Fifth House Ltd.
A Fitzhenry & Whiteside Company
1511, 1800-4 St. SW
Calgary, Alberta T2S 2S5

1-800-387-9776
www.fitzhenry.ca
Printed in China

ACKNOWLEDGEMENTS

There are many people who have encouraged and inspired me in my work as a naturalist. Special thanks to Denell Falk and her staff at *Civilized Adventures*. Without them, I wouldn't have explored so many unique places on Earth. They have been pivotal, in fact, in developing our very successful *ZooFari Travel Program* at the Calgary Zoo. We have been partners for nearly 20 years now, and this partnership has allowed my wanderlust to flourish! Thanks also to Andrew Prossin of *Peregrine Adventures* and all his staff. It's been an honour and a privilege to travel with such professionals to both ends of the earth, through rough seas and thick ice. I have learned so much from all of you, and I look forward to continuing a long relationship involving penguins, whales, and krill. And thanks to Jane Whitney and Steve Smith of *Whitney & Smith Legendary Expeditions,* who have taken me by kayak and foot to their best kept secrets in some of the most pristine polar regions. Thanks also to Pete Jess of *Jessco Operations* who developed *Arctic Watch Lodge.* Your enthusiasm for remote places is infectious.

A very special thanks to you, Carl Hrenchuck, my first hiking partner in the High Arctic. Our 4 months on Ellesmere Island a quarter century ago was an important turning point in my life, and you were a major part of that. It's time we plan another polar adventure together. Thank you, too, to the Calgary Zoo, for allowing my childhood dreams to come true. All of these evolved from endless hours spent in the woods, on the rivers, in the prairies, on the oceans, and high in the mountains.

I would also like to thank the people who have come on these trips with me. You have been wonderful traveling companions. And most importantly, I would like to thank my wife Dee, who shares my passion for these polar regions and who has been my most intrepid travel mate.